The Visible Signs of Scouting

In addition to Scouting's principles and training methods, there are at least four 'visible' signs which link the Movement round the world.

1. The Scout Badge

The World Badge, shown here, is being adopted by more and more countries as their membership badge. This badge is now the membership badge of Scouts in the United Kingdom.

2. The Scout Handshake

Scouts everywhere greet each other with the *left* handshake as a sign of their friendship and trust for one another.

3. The Scout S

is made by Scouts
uniform on certain formal oc
such as fla

4. The Scout Sign

is used when a Scout makes his Promise. The three fingers of the Salute and Sign remind a Scout of the three parts of the Promise.

INDEX

	Page
The Founder of the Scout Movement	4
Baden-Powell—the Soldier	6
The First Scout Camp	6
The growth of Scouting and Guiding	8
How a boy becomes a Scout	10
The Scout Promise and the Scout Law	12
Extension Activities	14
The Patrol and the Troop	16
The Patrol Leaders' Council	16
The Scout Family	18, 20
The Chief Scout	20
Scouting moves with the times	22
Training in the U.K.	24
The Progress Scheme	26 - 30
The Scout Proficiency Badge Scheme	32
Proficiency Badges	34
The Service Flash	34
Sea Activities	36
Air Activities	38
Scouting in Action	40, 42
National Scout Activity Centres	44
Other Outdoor Centres	44
Gilwell Park	46
Camp Sites	46
The International Scene	48
Jamborees	48
World Scouting	48, 50

SCOUTS
Who they are and what they do

by DAVID HARWOOD

with illustrations by
JOHN BERRY

Publishers: Wills & Hepworth Ltd Loughborough
First published 1971 © *Printed in England*

The Founder of the Scout Movement

Robert Stephenson Smyth Baden-Powell was born on February 22nd, 1857. Three years later his father died, and Mrs. Baden-Powell was left to bring up ten children.

At school Robert was neither an outstanding scholar nor sportsman, but he was a first-class marksman, a natural actor and artist, and he possessed a lively sense of humour. But sometimes he went off alone to an out-of-bounds woodland near the school, where he tracked and observed wildlife. "It brought some realisation of the wonders that surround us," he wrote later, "and it revealed too, through open eyes, the beauties of the woods and the sunsets."

In the holidays the Baden-Powell brothers went exploring, sailing boats which they had repaired themselves; hiking; camping-out in barns or in the open; visiting castles, buildings, factories and workshops. Robert did not know what he wanted to do when he left school. Unknown to his family, he took an army entrance examination and, much to everyone's surprise he passed so well that he was immediately commissioned as an officer.

He proved to be a brilliant soldier and was rapidly promoted. His unconventional training methods, of dividing his men into small groups and teaching them with competitions and games, were most successful.

4   *The young Baden-Powell observing wild life*

0 7214 0284 4

Baden-Powell – the Soldier

Probably Colonel Baden-Powell's best-known military success was when, with 1,000 of his men, he was surrounded by 9,000 Boers in the small town of Mafeking in South Africa.

Mafeking held out for 217 days until reinforcements came. In Britain everyone had followed the news from the besieged town with much interest. His remarkable achievement made him a national hero. In 1903, when only 46, B-P (as we shall call him) was appointed to be the army's youngest-ever Inspector-General of Cavalry.

A few years before, he had written a booklet called *Aids to Scouting*. This outlined his army training methods and was published in England during the Mafeking seige. On his return to England, B-P was amazed to find that boys had bought copies and, calling themselves Boy Scouts, had formed small groups to practise scoutcraft. B-P decided that he would revise the booklet to make it more suitable for young people, and by the summer of 1907 he was ready to put his ideas to the test.

The First Scout Camp

In August B-P, with a few adult helpers, set up camp on Brownsea Island in Poole Harbour, Dorset. His 'guinea pigs' were 20 boys from all walks of life. In those days only the army went to camp, so it *was* a great experiment. B-P divided the boys into Patrols with an older boy in charge of each. During the camp the boys had the time of their lives—swimming, stalking, hiking, playing games and, around the nightly campfire, listening to B-P telling stories of his adventures.

*The Stone on Brownsea Island
commemorating the first Scout Camp*

The growth of Scouting and Guiding

When the camp came to an end, B-P had proved that the most effective way to learn scoutcraft was through practices and games and that, when put on their honour, boys would usually do their very best. He completed writing *Scouting for Boys*, which was published in fortnightly instalments in 1908 and which he imagined would be used by existing youth organisations, schools, etc. He had no intention of founding a *new* youth movement. However, the book was an immediate best-seller and boys themselves formed Scout Troops. Soon Scouting spread overseas.

B-P was still an army officer but had to open an office to answer the hundreds of letters sent to him by Boy Scouts. In 1909 King Edward VII knighted B-P for his outstanding military career and especially for founding Scouting.

Girls had been joining too. With his sister, B-P devised a scheme for them, and in 1910 the Girl Guide Movement started. That same year B-P retired from the army to devote all his time and energy to Scouting. In 1912 he married Olave St. Claire Soames who shared his keen interest in young people. In 1918 she was elected Chief Guide, and at the 1st International Jamboree in 1920 B-P was acclaimed 'Chief Scout of the World'.

Together the two 'Chiefs' actively ensured the development of the Movements in the U.K. and travelled all over the world, helping and encouraging the growth of Scouting and Guiding. In 1929 King George V made B-P a peer and he became Lord Baden-Powell of Gilwell. B-P served Scouting until he died in 1941 at the age of 83. Lady B-P continued as World Chief Guide. All Scouts and Guides especially think of these two great people on February 22nd each year—their joint birthday.

The two 'Chiefs'

How a boy becomes a Scout

A boy becomes a Scout either by going up from the Cub Scout Pack or by joining a Scout Troop at any time between the ages of 11 and 16. He need *not* have been a Cub Scout to become a Scout. A Cub Scout already knows quite a lot about Scouting and probably has gained the Link Badge. This means he completed most of the requirements of the Scout Badge—which involves having a general knowledge of the Scout Movement and the development of world-wide Scouting, taking part in a Patrol or Troop activity out-of-doors, and understanding and accepting the Scout Promise and Law. So the Cub Scout already knows his Scout Leader, Patrol Leader and the other Scouts, and has had a glimpse of what they do. He then re-makes his Promise at a short, simple, sincere ceremony.

The 'direct entrant' (a boy who has not been a Cub Scout) attends a few Troop and/or Patrol Meetings and sees for himself what the great game of Scouting is all about. Once he decides that Scouting is for him and has gained the Scout Badge, he is invested.

There are thousands of Scout Troops throughout the country, so it is more than likely that there is one within reach of every boy. If he does not know a Scout or Leader in a Group he (or his parents) can either ask the local Youth Service Officer or write to the Secretary at Scout Headquarters who will give him the name and address of the local Troop.

A 'direct entrant' and a Cub Scout chat with their future Scout Leader

The Scout Promise and the Scout Law

On the opposite page you can read the Scout Promise and the Scout Law. They are very important, not only because of what they say and mean but also because all Scouting is based upon them. Remember, the only condition for a boy becoming a Scout is that he must make the Promise and understand the Law.

Honour and trust are closely linked. A person's honour is the standard by which he lives his life, and is worth only the value he himself gives it. A Promise is an agreement to do (or not to do) something. As far as Scouting is concerned the Promise is a promise for life. The Scout Promise and Law have three particularly notable features. First, keeping the Promise is the Scout's own responsibility: Scouting trusts the individual. Second, the Scout Law is positive: each part is a statement of what a Scout *is*. Third, they both set down ideals which, because no-one is 'perfect', everyone falls short of at one time or another. However, a Scout promises to *do his best* to keep both the Promise and the Law, and this is a lifelong challenge . . . and, of course, only he will know that he *is* doing his very best.

Every Scout in the world makes a similar Promise and lives by a similar Law. The 'World Brotherhood of Scouts' is a matter of fact, of which the Law and the Promise are the cornerstones. The actual words might vary between one country and another, but their meaning and spirit are the same.

Scouting is a world-wide brotherhood and this is the Promise and Law made by Scouts in the United Kingdom

The Scout Promise

On my honour I promise that I will do my best—

To do my duty to God and to the Queen

To help other people

And to keep the Scout Law

The Scout Law

1. A Scout is to be trusted
2. A Scout is loyal
3. A Scout is friendly and considerate
4. A Scout is a brother to all Scouts
5. A Scout has courage in all difficulties
6. A Scout makes good use of his time and is careful of possessions and property
7. A Scout has respect for himself and for others

Extension Activities

Some people have to bear mental or physical pain, perhaps through being born with a handicap, perhaps because of an accident. People with handicaps have to learn to re-adjust their lives and often prove their courage to those around them by the way they tackle activities that at first sight might seem impossible. How successfully they come to grips with their disabilities often depends on themselves.

A boy may have a handicap which prevents him from doing some activities but, providing he understands the Scout Law and makes the Scout Promise, he can become a Scout. Most Scouts with a handicap can do some things much better than other boys anyway! Scouting gives a boy with a handicap great opportunities to find his own limits and to develop his own skills, talents and interests within the Scout family. Thousands of boys and young men have proved, through Scouting, that they have the courage and determination to do their best to make the most of their lives.

Wherever possible a boy with a handicap joins a local Troop, even if he is home-bound. In some places, and in many special schools and hospitals, there are Groups which cater especially for those with handicaps, but again the boys are encouraged to take part in meetings with Patrols and Troops in the surrounding area.

*A Scout with a handicap
draws with a pen held between his toes*

The Patrol and the Troop

On page 6 you read that, at B-P's first Scout camp on Brownsea Island, the boys formed Patrols with an older boy, known as a Patrol Leader, in charge of each. "This organisation was the secret of our success," B-P wrote. "Each Patrol Leader was given full responsibility for the behaviour of his Patrol at all times . . The Patrol was the unit for work or play." Although the scope and variety of Scout training and activities is much greater today than it was when Scouting started, the Patrol System is still the basis of successful Scouting.

In a Patrol there are 4-8 Scouts and they are a real *team* in which each member, from the youngest to the Patrol Leader, has a job to do. Patrol-in-Council Meetings are informal get-togethers where each Scout has the chance to help plan the Patrol's programme and prepare the Patrol for action, and action is the keynote of Scouting. A Scout Troop is therefore *made up* of— and NOT *divided into*—Patrols.

The Patrol Leaders' Council

All Patrol Leaders in a Troop are members of the Patrol Leaders' Council, the Chairman of which is either the Senior Patrol Leader or each Patrol Leader in turn. The Scout Leader and his Assistants are also members, but they are there mainly as advisers and to keep everyone informed of Troop, District, County, National and other events, so that the Troop as a whole runs smoothly. The functions of the Council are: maintaining standards, guarding the reputation of the Troop and planning for the future, so each Patrol Leader does have real responsibilities both in his Patrol and in his Troop.

A Patrol Leaders' Council in session

The Scout Family

A Group is the basic 'family' unit in Scouting, with a Group Scout Leader at its head. In it there are usually at least one Cub Scout Pack for boys between the ages of 8 and 11, a Scout Troop for those aged 11 to 16, and a Venture Scout Unit for young men from 16 to 20. Often, however, a Venture Scout Unit draws on more than one Group for its members. Each Section has its own trained Leaders who are called Scouters.

A number of Groups in a locality form a District with the District Commissioner at its head, and several Districts make up a County under the leadership of a County Commissioner, who is the Chief Scout's personal representative.

In addition to the Scouters there are many other people who help Scouting at all levels; some, like the Assistant County and District Commissioners, are uniformed, others who are called 'lay' helpers and officers are not. The latter include parents and friends of Scouting who work very hard to raise funds, to maintain headquarters, to assist as instructors and examiners, to look after the paperwork, and in many other ways to enable the Scouters to concentrate on their 'job', which is Scouting for boys.

The Headquarters of the Scout Association is at 25 Buckingham Palace Road, London, S.W.1. Some of the Headquarters staff are voluntary (i.e. they have other jobs and are not paid for the work they do for Scouting), others are full-time professionals. All *serve* and *advise*: they do not *dictate*.

A 'Gang Show' organised to raise funds for the Movement

The Scout Family *(continued)*

The Council of the Scout Association is the governing body of the Movement in the U.K. The members are the voluntary Headquarters Commissioners, all the County Commissioners, a nominated 'lay' person from each County and elected members of distinction from public life.

The Chief Scout

The Chief Scout is appointed by the Council. The only person who has been Chief Scout of the World was B-P. Since Scouting started the Chief Scouts of the U.K. and Commonwealth have been:

Lord Baden-Powell	1908 - 1941
Lord Somers	1941 - 1944
Lord Rowallan	1945 - 1959

The present Chief Scout, Lord Maclean, was appointed in 1959. He was a Cub himself when he was a boy. He lives at Duart Castle, the ancient stronghold of the Clan Maclean on the Isle of Mull off the west coast of Scotland. The Chief spends many months each year travelling in the United Kingdom, meeting boys and Leaders, as well as taking a keen and active part in all aspects of Scouting today. The Chief makes regular visits abroad each year and in the first eleven years of his appointment completed visits to all major Branches of the Movement in the Commonwealth. The Chief Scout was created a Life Peer by Her Majesty the Queen in the 1971 New Year Honours List.

Scouting moves with the times

Times have changed since B-P founded Scouting, yet the Movement is still strong. It has progressed with the times and has adapted its programmes and training to the needs of boys and young men wherever they are and without in any way abandoning its principles.

As you will read later, Scouting has many 'ingredients' which, by providing enjoyable and appealing programmes based on the Promise and the Law and guided by trained adult leadership, encourage each Scout's physical, mental and spiritual development so that he can become a useful and reliable citizen.

The Scouts' Motto is 'Be Prepared' which they apply to everything they do. They are trained to be prepared to look after themselves, to help other people, to be adventurous, to learn skills, to understand, respect and enjoy the great outdoors, to develop their talents and interests. Scout training is not an end in itself . . . it is practical, it encourages a boy to follow his religion, it has a sense of purpose and—above all—it is FUN! In Scouting, training and activities go together.

Pony-trekking can be a Scout activity

Training in the U.K.

Most of a Scout's training is by *doing* things, not by sitting through long lessons nor by just studying books . . . though that does not mean a Scout does not listen and cannot read! Training and activities go together. The series of Scout tests in the U.K. forms the Progress Scheme which provides a boy with a variety of challenges. His Patrol Leader and Scouters, Instructors, experts and other helpers are all there to teach, guide and show him 'how'. He will also learn a lot from experience—and from his mistakes!

In the U.K. each Scout is encouraged to have his own Progress Book which lists the full details of the Progress Scheme.

Special Note: In the next few pages there is an outline of the requirements for the Progress Scheme. The requirements may be met in any order and at any time convenient to the individual Scout so that he can take advantage of opportunities as and when they arise. In this way a Scout may meet the requirements of a section of the Chief Scout's Award in his first few months in the Troop, but he cannot be presented with the Advanced Scout Standard until he has completed all the requirements of the Scout Standard and must wait until he has completed all that is necessary for the Advanced Scout Standard before receiving the Chief Scout's Award.

Scouts learning to fence with expert instruction

The Progress Scheme

1. Attaining the Scout Standard

 A Scout learns about such practical activities as basic First Aid, how to pack a rucsac, map reading, fire-lighting, outdoor cooking, how to use a knife and an axe, and all about the Country Code so that he can go hiking and camping. He learns something about his neighbourhood and shows some proficiency or skill in a hobby or interest.

Most of these requirements are included in a Patrol's or Troop's normal programme. The older Scouts teach the younger ones and a Patrol Leader does the testing. The Badge is awarded on the recommendation of the Patrol Leaders' Council.

2. Attaining the Advanced Scout Standard

 The Advanced Scout Standard increases a Scout's knowledge of camping, First Aid, 'emergency' action and service to others. It gives him the chance to broaden the scope of his activities. In a number of the requirements he is given a choice.

He learns to swim, becomes more proficient with map and compass, and knows what safety precautions to take so he can then go on such adventurous activities as hill-walking, abseiling, sailing, canoeing and cross-country expeditions. He keeps a nature diary, weather record or the Patrol Log over a period of time. He makes a report on a local feature, or surveys a small area near his home, and/or passes a Pursuit Proficiency Badge (see p. 32).

Scouts on a hike

The Progress Scheme *(continued)*

The tests' requirements are met through arrangements made by the Scout Leader. Before the Badge is awarded the Scout discusses his understanding of the Scout Promise and Law, and his further Scout Training, with his Scout Leader.

3. Attaining the Chief Scout's Award

 The aim of every Scout is the Chief Scout's Award, which is the hallmark of a trained and competent Scout. There are three main parts to the Award—Achievement, Leadership, Responsibility.

(a) ACHIEVEMENT. The choice of activities is so great that only an outline is given here. A Scout cannot take those activities which he did for his Scout Standard and Advanced Scout Standard badges. He reaches a set standard in FOUR of the activities listed below, but the four must include at least one skill from *three* of the Groups.

GROUP A: CHALLENGE. Canoeing or sailing; mountaineering or rock-climbing; water ski-ing; snow ski-ing; gliding.

GROUP B: PRACTICAL. Car maintenance; karting; amateur radio; domestic electrics; carpentry; metal work; house maintenance; photography.

GROUP C: ENDEAVOUR. Survival; outdoor sport or outdoor interest; expedition on foot, by bicycle, canoe or boat, or a night hike; personal survival; swimming; indoor sport.

GROUP D: SOCIAL. Helping to organise and run a mixed activity; cooking; camping abroad or with Scouts from overseas; successfully completing a residential course; entertaining.

Learning about car maintenance
for the Chief Scout's Award

28

The Progress Scheme *(continued)*

(b) LEADERSHIP. So that he has the necessary technical knowledge to teach younger Scouts, he must have the Advanced Scout Standard Badge. He then puts his knowledge into practice by training at least two Scouts to Advanced Scout Standard in two activities. He may, as an alternative, satisfactorily complete a course of Patrol Leader training and guide at least one member of his Patrol through the Scout Standard.

He will also show his ability as a leader in a practical way like organising a Patrol camp or activity, helping to organise and run a Troop activity, or training and leading a team of 'casualties' for First Aid training.

(c) RESPONSIBILITY. A Scout arranges and does a useful voluntary service project which requires *regular* attendance over a period of at least three months. He passes one Service and one Pursuit Badge, (see p. 34) after passing the Advanced Scout Standard, or gains a particular qualification with an approved organisation (for example, the Royal Life Saving Society, British Canoe Union, etc.).

He also shows his acceptance of responsibility at home, church, Troop, school or place of work.

The Chief Scout's Award is awarded by the District Commissioner on the recommendation of the Scout Leader, and the certificate is usually presented by the County Commissioner at a reception.

Camera instruction from an expert

The Scout Proficiency Badge Scheme

The word 'proficiency' means 'expertness', and through the scheme of Proficiency Badges a Scout can increase his knowledge or skills in particular subjects. They give him opportunities to reach much higher standards than the 'general' training he receives in the Progress Scheme.

From the illustrations of all the badges at the back of this book, you can see that there is a very wide choice of subjects, and in many badges there are a number of alternatives. In some cases a Scout attains the requirements by himself, in others his Group or District will organise special badge courses, in others he will automatically qualify for all, or part, of a badge by passing an examination or test of another organisation (for example, to gain the Ambulance Badge he gains the 'Essentials of First Aid' Certificate of the St. John Ambulance Association *or* the Junior Certificate of the British Red Cross Society).

Scouting wants its members to 'look wide' and, particularly with specialised activities, encourages them to join a specialist club, society, etc. In this way Scouts not only get the very best information and instruction but also their knowledge of particular subjects is of immense value to their Patrol, Troop and Group, for no Scout Leader can possibly be an expert in everything included in Scouting!

A Scout enjoys fishing with an Angling Club

Proficiency Badges *(see endpapers)*

There are four groups of Proficiency Badges.

Interest Badges have relatively easy requirements and are primarily intended for younger Scouts.

Pursuit Badges are of a practical nature.

Service Badges are intended mainly for older Scouts. The standards expected are 'absolute', which means that they cannot be varied because of a boy's age or ability, and they include practical application as well as theory.

Instructor Badges in certain subjects are for the Scout who has specialised in a particular field by gaining the appropriate Pursuit, Interest or Service Proficiency Badge, and who has then been trained to instruct members of the Movement in the technical skills involved. A Scout may not gain more than two Instructor Badges, which have a red background and a gold border.

The Service Flash

A Service Flash on a Scout's uniform is just one way of showing that he has been—and is—keeping his Scout Promise 'to help other people'. He will either hold the Advanced Scout Standard or be at least 14; he will have gained two Service Proficiency Badges (or a badge from the Interest or Pursuit Group may count as *one* of the two if he is carrying out regular service under the heading of the badge, e.g. acting as the Troop Librarian or being a member of his church's bell-ringing team); he will have passed an Instructor Proficiency Badge, and he will have put his training for a Service or Instructor Badge into practice by giving regular service over a period of at least three months (averaging about an hour a week) *after* gaining the badge.

Practising the techniques of life-saving

Sea Activities

Sea Scout Troops may operate wherever there is water deep enough for a boat to float.

Sea Scouts take part in the normal Scout Progress Scheme but they also have special training in water-borne activities. This special training, and the badges, are available to Scouts other than Sea Scouts.

Boatman Badge

For this a Scout must already have the Scout Standard Badge and then learn something of the preparation and practice of boating and take part in a project afloat.

Coxwain's Mate Badge

For this a Scout must already have the Advanced Scout Standard Badge and have an understanding of the correct approach to boating (e.g. rules and signals, capsize drill and weather forecasting), take part in activities on the water and assist with boat maintenance and be a member of a crew on a 24-hour expedition in a rowing boat.

Coxwain Badge

In addition to having the Advanced Scout Standard Badge, to attain this badge a Scout must know about such things as how to chart and plot a position, about communications at sea (buoys, lights and signals), weather, personal survival, boat repairs and taking charge of a boat and crew for emergency drills. He will also go on an expedition under sail or power covering at least 10 nautical miles with a night in camp or aboard. Opportunities are given for experience in powered craft, instruction in navigation and offshore cruising in larger craft.

Sea Scouter's
Cap Badge

Air Activities

Air Scouts take the normal Progress Scheme with additional aeronautical subjects. The special training, and the badges, are available to all Scouts.

Airman Badge

To obtain this badge, a Scout must gain the Scout Standard Badge. He must have a basic knowledge of aircraft, and demonstrate some aircraft manoeuvres using a model, stick glider.

Senior Airman Badge

In addition to gaining the Advanced Scout Standard Badge, for this badge a Scout must increase his practical and theoretical knowledge of aviation. He learns how a parachute works, what aircraft marshalling signals are, how the weather affects air activities, and how to read air maps. He can specialise in one of the following subjects—aircraft recognition, airline operation, aerospace, military or private aviation. He builds a model aircraft and flies in an aircraft other than as a fare-paying passenger.

Master Airman Badge

A Scout must possess the Advanced Scout Standard Badge. He then learns the basic rules for flying in light aircraft or gliders and understands the system of controlled air spaces. He is taught the principles of flight, how piston and jet engines work and how to prepare an air chart. He reaches a higher standard in one of the five subjects given in the Senior Airman above. On a practical level he will pilot a dual-controlled powered aircraft or glider, *or* undertake an advanced research project.

Learning about aircraft

Scout Wings

Scouting in Action

Almost all Scout activities are based on the Patrol because the Patrol is *the* unit in Scouting, with the Patrol Leader taking a real part in the planning and running of activities. This does not mean that each Patrol works only on its own. Patrols come together for Troop Meetings and activities. Scouts from different Patrols may work for a particular Proficiency Badge in which they share a common interest. Older Scouts in the Troop will take part in adventurous activities suited to their age (for example, mountaineering, survival expeditions and caving).

Scouting is essentially an outdoor Movement and, even when the weather prevents Scouts going outside, they will almost certainly be getting ready for outdoor activities. No two Scout programmes are the same from year to year or between one Troop and another.

Variety is another feature of Scouting. While the majority of the 'traditional' Scout activities like hiking, camping and pioneering are still included, the range and scope of activities and pursuits in Scouting today include cyclo-cross, radio construction, water and snow ski-ing, trampolining, home decorating, folk groups, and so on. Scouts are encouraged to pursue whatever interests and talents they have within Scouting (providing, of course, they do not conflict with the Promise and the Law).

Cyclo-cross—another Scout activity

Scouting in Action *(continued)*

In addition to the Patrol and Troop programmes, Scouts have opportunities to take part in activities with the Girl Guides, as well as those organised by the Youth Service. There are also Scout events and competitions organised at District, County and National levels at which Scouts have the chance to meet other Scouts.

A particular highlight in the National Scout Calendar is the St. George's Day Parade and Service at Windsor, where Queen's Scouts march through the Castle quadrangle and then join together in an act of worship in St. George's Chapel.

There are other national and international 'dates' in a Scout's diary. For example, Scout Job Week in the spring is when all members of the Movement in the U.K. can earn funds for their Group by doing jobs of work.

Each year thousands of Scouts in all corners of the world make contact with each other via amateur radio in the international Jamboree-on-the-Air.

Enjoying the thrills of a karting competition

National Scout Activity Centres

To help Scouts make the most of their opportunities for adventure, Scout Headquarters has established Activity Centres, staffed by expert instructors. At the Air Activity Centre at Lasham, Hampshire, there are facilities for gliding, power-flying and parascending. At the Boating Activity Centre, Longridge, near Marlow, Buckinghamshire, there is scope for sailing, power-boating and canoeing. The first full-time caving centre was established by the Scout Association at Whernside Manor, Dentdale in the West Riding of Yorkshire. This Centre also covers Field Studies and Mountaineering.

Other Outdoor Centres

There are many other special Centres which can be used by all Scouts. Here are just five examples—Welsh Scouts have an excellent climbing centre in Snowdonia; at Lochgoilhead the Scottish Scout Headquarters has an Adventure and Boating Centre; in the North Riding of Yorkshire the Watson Scout Centre in Carlton-in-Cleveland is ideal for mountaineering, gliding, pony trekking and canoeing; Hertfordshire Scouts' Hill Station in Perthshire caters for all kinds of mountaincraft, as well as sailing, canoeing and water ski-ing; near Plymouth, the Dewerstone Centre, owned by Devon Scouts, provides a base for rock climbing, hiking and exploration on southern Dartmoor.

Gilwell Park

This 108 acre estate on the edge of Epping Forest, north-east of London, is the U.K. Scouts' Adult Leader Training Centre and the principal International Centre for Research and Experimentation in Training methods. It also has excellent facilities for camping, and during the year organises many events for all sections of the Scout Movement, such as the National Father and Son Camp, National Scout Family Camp, Cub Scout Day, Sedan Chair Rally, and so on.

Camp Sites

As well as the Activity Centres, Scout Headquarters owns some permanent camp sites which have been especially developed for Scouts. Each has a full-time warden. Most of these sites have facilities for training (many run Proficiency Badge courses) and all provide excellent places for a Patrol or a Troop camp.

Most Scout Counties and numerous Scout Districts and Groups have their own permanent camp sites.

All over the country private individuals allow camping on their land, and many will permit only Scouts because they know that Scouts set high standards of camping.

Exploring underground caves

The International Scene

With more than 13 million members in over 150 countries, Scouting *is* a world-wide Movement. U.K. Scouts prove this for themselves in many ways by having pen friends, link-ups between Patrols and Troops in other countries, and camps and expeditions abroad.

Each year about 16,000 U.K. Scouts seek adventure overseas. Wherever they go they meet other Scouts and find that the Scout Badge and the Left Handshake are international passports to friendship and goodwill.

Many Scouts from other lands visit the U.K. too. For example, in a year more than 10,000 Scouts of upwards of 40 nationalities stay at Baden-Powell House, the U.K. Scouts' social and residential centre in West London. Thousands more camp in all parts of the country.

Jamborees

Each year many countries organise a National Jamboree ('a large gathering of Scouts') to which overseas Scouts are usually invited. Every four years there is a World Jamboree where Scouts from all over the globe get together for a full programme of events as well as informal chats, badge-swopping, and so on. In 1967 a large contingent of U.K. Scouts were among the 15,000 who went to the 12th World Jamboree in the U.S.A. Japan was selected as the country in which to hold the 13th World Jamboree in 1971.

World Scouting

The Boy Scouts' World Conference is composed of all National Member Associations, each having six delegates. The Conference is World Scouting's 'General Assembly' and meets every two years.

A Scout camp in Africa

World Scouting *(continued)*

The Boy Scouts' World Committee consists of 12 men from 12 countries. It is elected by the Conference and meets regularly between the two-yearly conferences.

The Boy Scouts' World Bureau is the permanent secretariat of the World Conference and Committee. The Bureau has about 20 staff, most of whom work at the Headquarters in Geneva, but there are Regional Offices in Mexico, the Philippines, Syria and Nigeria. The Bureau helps National Associations to improve their Scouting, through visits and by correspondence. The staff also organises such events as the Jamboree-on-the-Air and World Jamborees.

The Scout Universal Fund, which is administered by the World Bureau and is known as the Scout 'U' Fund, is an example of the fourth Scout Law ('A Scout is a Brother to all Scouts') in action. Its aims are to give all Scouts throughout the world a chance to share in making Scouting available to a large number of boys and to strengthen the international brotherhood of Scouting. It helps Scouts to help themselves by providing money for books, camps, training centres and equipment. It assists Scouts in distress and brings Scouting to less fortunate boys—the orphans and those with a handicap.

Scouting makes life happier for some blind boys

PURSUIT
Proficiency Badges

Specimen
INSTRUCTOR'S
Badge